FRANKIE'S
MAGIC
FOOTBALL

BY FRANK LAMPARD

FRANKIE'S MAGIC FOOTBALL

FRANKIE VS THE MUMMY'S MENACE
FRANK LAMPARD

LITTLE, BROWN BOOKS FOR YOUNG READERS
www.lbkids.co.uk

LITTLE, BROWN BOOKS FOR YOUNG READERS

First published in Great Britain in 2014 by
Little, Brown Books for Young Readers

5 7 9 10 8 6 4

A CIP catalogue record for this book
is available from the British Library.

978-0-349-00163-0

Typeset in Cantarell by M Rules
Printed and bound in Great Britain by
Clays Ltd, St Ives plc

Papers used by LBYR are from well-managed forests
and other responsible sources.

MIX
Paper from
responsible sources
FSC® C104740

Little, Brown Books for Young Readers
An imprint of
Little, Brown Book Group
100 Victoria Embankment
London EC4Y 0DY

An Hachette UK Company
www.hachette.co.uk

www.lbkids.co.uk

To my mum Pat, who encouraged me to do my homework in between kicking a ball all around the house, and is still with me every step of the way.

*Welcome to a fantastic
Fantasy League – the greatest
football competition ever held
in this world or any other!*

*You'll need four on a team,
so choose carefully. This is a lot
more serious than a game in the
park. You'll never know who your
next opponents will be, or
where you'll face them.*

*So lace up your boots, players,
and good luck! The whistle's
about to blow!*

The Ref

CHAPTER 1

Frankie stood in front of the marble statue. He checked the question on his sheet.

"Who ruled the Roman Empire in 60 AD?"

He read the little card on the wall.

The Emperor Nero (ruled 54–68 AD).

Wow! he thought. *That's nearly two thousand years ago!*

He wrote the answer: 'Nero.'

Frankie heard the shuffle of footsteps and turned to see Charlie dragging his feet along the ground. He was carrying his clipboard in his hands.

"The museum is the most boring place in the universe," said Frankie's friend.

"More boring than Maths lessons with Ms Brown?" asked Frankie, grinning.

"OK, the *second* most boring place," said Charlie. "I can't believe they cancelled football practice for this." He flopped onto the bottom step of a set of stairs, tossed the clipboard aside, and rested his chin in his gloved hands. Frankie saw Charlie had filled in some of the answers, but not many.

"Ahem!" said a voice. Mr Donald strode out from behind another statue. "Charles, I don't see how you're going to complete your answer-sheet unless you take those goalkeeping gloves off."

Frankie saw his friend quickly hide his clipboard. "I've done all the answers, sir," said Charlie.

"Really?" said Mr Donald, narrowing his eyes. "I don't see

how that's possible. You haven't even visited the Egyptian gallery yet and we have to leave in fifteen minutes."

Charlie blushed. "Just going now, sir," he said. With a sigh he stood up and began to climb the stairs.

"Wait for me," said Frankie. "I'm finished with the Roman questions."

"Good, good," said Mr Donald. "Your friend Louise is already up there. Almost done, I believe."

"She would be!" grumbled Charlie.

As they followed the sign to the

Egyptian gallery, they passed the café. Loud shouts and laughter came from inside. A moment later, Frankie's brother Kevin and his friends spilled out. When his eyes landed on Frankie, he stopped laughing and sneered.

"It's the Geek Squad!" he said. "Have you answered all Donaldo's questions yet?"

"Just keep walking," Frankie whispered to Charlie. He'd hoped he wouldn't bump into his brother's class. They were at the museum too, researching their history projects.

Frankie and Charlie found Louise

in the Egyptian room inspecting a green jar on a glass shelf. "This belonged to a Pharaoh," she said, when she spotted them.

"A Fair-what?" asked Charlie.

Louise rolled her eyes. "The Pharaoh was the name ancient Egyptians gave their king," she said.

"Yeah, I knew that," mumbled Charlie.

"This jar was used to put their heart in after they were mummified," said Louise.

"Yuck!" said Frankie. He checked his question sheet. "We have to find the name of five Egyptian

Gods," he added. "Apparently the Egyptians worshipped more than sixty!"

"I've got four already," said Louise. She grinned and hid her answer sheet as Charlie peered over her shoulder. "Find your own!"

Frankie wasn't interested in Louise's answers. He was looking at something in the centre of the room, cordoned off with a red rope. It was like an open coffin, standing on its end. The lid was decorated with the face and body of a man. He wore a colourful head-dress, painted gold and red, and he had a strange, thin beard. Across his clothes were hundreds of tiny symbols.

"Check that out," he said.

"That's the mummy's sarcophagus," said Louise.

"Sark–Off–A–What?" asked Charlie.

"Like a coffin," said Louise. "When a pharaoh died, his body was preserved as a mummy, then the mummy was put in a pyramid, inside a sarcophagus."

Frankie marvelled at the amazing painted details.

The card next to the exhibit read: SARCOPHAGUS OF UNKNOWN PHARAOH.

I wonder what all the little pictures mean," said Charlie.

"They're called hieroglyphs," said Louise.

"Hire–Oh–What?" said Charlie, smiling. "Only kidding."

Frankie peered even closer, right into the golden eyes of the unknown king. Then he felt his bag strap snag on his shoulder, almost pulling him off his feet. He spun round to see Kevin holding his bag.

"Hey! I'm not finished with you, little brother."

"Give that back," said Frankie, deadly serious.

"Ooh . . . scary!" said his brother.

He undid the zip on Frankie's bag and tipped it upside down. Out fell Frankie's pencil case, his lunchbox, his books. And, last of all, his battered football. He dropped the bag at Frankie's feet.

"Pass it here!" said Kev's friend, Liam.

Before Frankie could react, Kev back-heeled the ball to Liam.

"Don't be idiots!" said Louise. "You'll break something!"

"What are you scared of?" asked Kev's friend, Matt. "The mummy's curse?"

Charlie went to get the ball, but Liam chipped it over his shoulder to Rob. All Kevin's friends were laughing. Frankie stuffed his things in his bag and sprang to his feet.

"Come and get your rubbish ball," said Rob, stepping over it.

Frankie ran at him, his blood pumping. Rob tried to go around him, but Frankie kept his eye on the ball and tackled him. The ball spun up into the air, straight towards the ancient green jar.

Frankie, and everyone else, sucked in a breath.

The ball just missed the jar and rolled under the rope towards the mummy's sarcophagus.

"What are you lot up to?" said a

voice over the silence. It was Mrs
Murray, Kevin's history teacher.
She might only be five feet tall
and about a hundred years old, but
Frankie knew they were terrified
of her. "Haven't you got work to be
doing?" she said.

Kevin and his mates all scarpered

quickly, muttering "Yes, Miss" and "Sorry, Miss".

Mrs Murray glared at Frankie, then followed them out of the room.

"Phew!" said Louise. "That jar is priceless!"

Frankie blew out a long breath and went to get his ball. He stopped right in his tracks when he saw the ball had somehow rolled *inside* the sarcophagus. "Weird," he said.

"What?" asked Charlie.

Frankie pointed at the sarcophagus. "Did you put it in there?"

Both Louise and Charlie shook their heads.

Frankie edged closer. He was going to have to step over the rope to get the ball. He looked up, checking for cameras. *If Mr Donald sees me, I'm going to be in deep trouble.*

As he lifted a leg over the rope, the painted gold eyes of the pharaoh watched him intently. Frankie didn't believe in a mummy's curse, but he couldn't help but shudder.

He reached out for the ball, heart thumping.

Then, with no one touching it, the sarcophagus lid snapped shut.

CHAPTER 2

Louise squealed and Frankie jerked his hand back.

"Is it supposed to do that?" Charlie asked. His skin was pale.

"There must have been a draft," said Frankie. "Help me get it open again."

"I'll keep look-out," said Louise.

She went to stand by the door, as Charlie jumped over the rope to Frankie's side. They each gripped the crack of the coffin lid and pulled. With a blast of hot air, they managed to prise it open.

"Not again!" Charlie groaned.

Frankie found a smile playing over his lips. There was no sign of the football in the sarcophagus, but instead there was a swirling doorway of colour.

"Time for another adventure," said Frankie.

Charlie frowned. "I'm not sure this time."

From her look-out position,

Louise gasped. "Donaldo's coming! Quick!" She rushed over, and hurled herself through the portal.

"Coming?" said Frankie.

"I guess I haven't got a choice any more," said Charlie. He leapt through after Louise.

"Where have you lot got to?" called Mr Donald. "The bus will be leaving in five minutes."

Frankie saw his teacher's shadow approaching down the corridor.

"Now or never," he muttered, and stepped into the sarcophagus.

"Aaargh!" Frankie was falling, tumbling over and over. Something gritty filled his mouth, drowning

his cries. The world was a blur. He couldn't see because his eyes were blinking madly.

He rolled to a halt on his back.

Frankie opened his eyes and saw the sun like a golden disc right overhead. The sky was the purest blue he'd ever seen, without a cloud in sight. He felt sand in his fingers.

"Where are we?" said Charlie.

Frankie sat up and saw an enormous sand dune rising above him.

"We're in the desert," he said, climbing to his feet and brushing down his clothes.

Only they weren't his clothes. Like Charlie, he was wearing a linen tunic, tied at the waist with a belt. Louise wore a blue dress which fell all the way to her ankles.

Frankie turned on the spot, but all he could see was more sand, stretching for miles.

"The magic football must have brought us here to play a game," he said.

Charlie spat out a mouthful of sand and shielded his eyes from the sun with a glove. "Maybe it's broken," he said, "because we're in the middle of nowhere."

"And we haven't got any water,"

said Louise. She looked down and yelped. "What's that?"

The sand by her feet was moving. Something was squirming around beneath the surface. A furry snout broke loose, followed by a dog's head.

"Max!" cried Frankie.

"Don't just stand there!" barked the little dog. "Help a hound out, why don't you?"

Frankie fell to his knees and started scooping sand away. Soon Max scrambled free and shook the sand out of his fur.

"Great," he said. "I was having a nice doze by the back door."

"The magic football must have fetched you," said Frankie, "even though you weren't with us in the museum."

"Fetched me where exactly?" asked Max.

Frankie shrugged. He set off up the side of the sand dune with the sun beating down on his head. The others traipsed after him, slipping and sliding on the loose sand.

As Frankie reached the crest of the dune, he gasped. In the distance, rising out of the desert, was an enormous pyramid. It blurred in the haze of heat rising from the ground.

"We're in ancient Egypt!" said
Louise.

"But where are our opponents?"
asked Charlie.

Frankie pointed to the pyramid.
"My guess is we'll find them over
there. Let's go!"

They trudged down the other

side of the dune towards the pyramid.

"It's bigger than I ever imagined," said Louise. "Did you know that the pyramids sometimes took more than twenty years to build? They had to drag the huge blocks of stone from the River Nile by hand. Some pyramids had over a million blocks."

"Whoa!" said Charlie. "That would be even more boring than maths."

Max was having trouble keeping up, because his paws kept sinking in the sand. Frankie stooped to pick him up. As he rose again, he saw a cart approaching, drawn by a camel.

The driver drew up alongside them and Frankie saw the cart was empty.

"What are you doing out here, wandering in the desert heat?" asked the man.

Frankie searched his mind for an answer, and decided on the truth.

"We're here for a game of football," he said.

"Aren't we all," said the man, settling back onto a large cushion. "Who are you supporting?"

"We're playing actually," said Frankie.

"We're Frankie's Fantasy FC," added Louise.

The man looked at them solemnly for a moment, and then burst out laughing.

"Very funny!" he said. "You almost had me there!"

"We're serious," said Charlie, holding up his hands. "Why do you think I'm wearing these?"

The man was serious again. "I'm not sure why you're wearing gloves in the desert," he said. "But a bunch of kids haven't got a snowball in the desert's chance of beating King Tut's team."

CHAPTER 3

Frankie looked at his friends. "Don't worry," he said. "We've played against plenty of tough opponents." But even he was secretly worried. "Can you take us to the pyramid?" he asked.

The man grinned. "Of course!" he said. "The name's Medhi. Hop on."

In a short while, they reached the side of the pyramid. Up close, it seemed even bigger, completely blocking out the sun in the sky. Hundreds of people gathered near a doorway, where two bare-chested guards with swords hanging at their sides were letting them in a few at a time.

"Where are they going?" asked Charlie. "Is it hollow?"

Louise shook her head. "No, but there are chambers and secret passageways inside."

"Cool!" said Frankie.

"You'd better get out here while I find somewhere to park

my camel," said Medhi. "Join the queue."

Frankie and his friends jumped out. The camel drew back its lips and hissed when it saw Max near its ankles.

"Don't mind her," Medhi said. "She's more of a cat lover. Doesn't like stray dogs."

"I'm no stray!" said Max. "I'm a house dog, thank you very much."

They walked over to the spectators waiting to get in. There were men and women, young and old. Some sheltered under parasols, while others wafted their faces with fans.

"We need to get inside and find the referee," said Frankie. He tapped a man on the shoulder. "Excuse me, can we come past, please?"

"No," said the man. "Wait your turn."

Frankie noticed that many of the people queuing were clutching rough pieces of paper, showing a line drawing of a man standing over a football. Frankie remembered from the museum that the Egyptians wrote on something called papyrus – paper made from river reeds.

"Any idea who the opponents

are today?" asked a woman with an elaborate hairstyle pinned up on her head.

"Nope," said a thin man, sipping from a water flask. "Who cares? They'll lose like all the others, and end up locked in the pyramid for eternity."

Charlie's eyes went wide. "Hang on? Isn't eternity a long time?"

"It's *forever*," said Louise.

"We're not going to lose," said Frankie. He looked around for Medhi, but he'd vanished.

At that moment, shouts went up at the back of the crowd and another guard came rushing through. He shouted, "Move! Make way for King Tut!"

A murmur passed through the queue and everyone shuffled aside. A row of servants approached, carrying a kind of couch on their shoulders. On top of the couch was a boy a bit older than Frankie, his chin raised proudly. Beside him sat a girl. They looked so alike that they had to be brother and sister. The servants carried them inside.

Eventually they reached the front of the queue.

"Tickets, please," said the bare-chested guard.

Frankie looked at Louise, but

she just shrugged. "We don't have tickets," he said.

The guard folded his beefy arms and glowered. "No tickets, no entry," he said.

"But we're here to play!" said Charlie.

The guard looked Charlie up and

down. Then he started laughing and gave his fellow guard a friendly slap on the shoulder. "Yes, and my brother is the God Anubis!" he said, tears pouring down his face.

"Hey!" said a woman's voice. "Where's my bracelet?"

Everyone, including Frankie, turned. The woman was feeling her wrist, frowning.

"And my ring's gone too!" said the man next to her. He narrowed his eyes. "There's a pickpocket around here."

His eyes settled on Frankie and his friends. Then so did everyone else's.

"It wasn't us . . ." said Louise.

Frankie heard the hiss of metal, as the guards drew their swords.

"Run!" he shouted.

They dashed out of the queue as the crowd erupted in shouting. Frankie didn't know which way to go, so he headed alongside the pyramid until his breath was coming hard and fast and his legs were aching. When he looked back, he saw that no one was following them.

Charlie had his hands on his knees, panting.

Max kicked up some sand. "It's like being at the beach, but there are no crabs to chase."

Frankie was wondering what to do next, when Louise pointed past him. "Isn't that Medhi?" she said.

Frankie saw him too. Medhi was standing at the base of the pyramid, running his fingers along the blocks as if he was looking for something.

"Hey!" said Frankie.

Medhi straightened up, blushing as they approached.

"Don't you have a ticket either?" asked Charlie.

"Something like that," grinned Medhi.

"What are you doing?" asked Louise.

Medhi's grin stayed fixed. "Oh,

you know, just sightseeing." He waved a hand at the surrounding area. As he did so, Frankie saw the flash of gold on his wrist. It was a bracelet he was sure Medhi hadn't been wearing before. Come to think of it, there was a silver ring on his finger too.

"You're the thief!" gasped Frankie.

"He's a tomb-robber, I'll bet," said Louise. "Looking to steal the pharaoh's treasure."

Medhi raised his finger to his lips. "Shhh! Anyway, what proof have you got?"

Max growled. "Maybe we should

summon those guards with the sharp swords?"

Medhi spread his hands. "No need for that, fellow travellers. Can't we do a deal?" He took the bracelet off his wrist and held it out to Louise.

Frankie was about to call the guards, when he had a better idea.

"Maybe we *can* do a deal," he said.

He saw Louise's eyes grow wide. "But he's a crook!" she said.

"Help us get inside the pyramid," said Frankie, "and we won't tell on you."

Charlie smiled. "Good thinking, Captain," he said.

Medhi stroked his chin and then nodded. "All right. I know there's a loose block here somewhere leading to a secret passage. We just have to find it."

Frankie gazed at the huge pyramid. "There must be thousands of stones!" he said.

But Max was already scampering through the sand, nose to the blocks. About halfway along, he paused. "Over here!" he barked.

Frankie and the others rushed over, including Medhi. Max rested his paws on the stone.

"How do you know it's the one?" asked the pickpocket.

"I can smell the air on the other side," said Max. "Not such a useless stray, after all, hey?"

Frankie and Louise set their shoulders against one side of the block. They strained against the stone, but it didn't budge.

"Are you sure?" Frankie asked Max.

"Come on, you weaklings," said the dog.

Charlie pressed both gloves against the block and joined the effort.

"You too!" said Frankie to Medhi.

The robber laid his back against the block.

"After three," said Frankie. "One . . . Two . . . Three!"

They all grunted and pushed. With a grinding sound, the rock slid into the pyramid, revealing a black passage beyond.

"We're in!" said Frankie.

CHAPTER 4

"You guys are naturals," said Medhi, rushing back and grabbing a sack from the sand.

"We're not thieves like you," said Louise, as she crept into the darkness. Frankie followed her with Max at his heels.

"Wait until you see the mummy's

mask!" said Medhi, heading in last. "It's solid gold and worth a fortune! You'll soon forget about football."

With only the sunlight from outside trickling into the passage, it was gloomy. But when Frankie's eyes began to adjust, he made out smooth carved walls and a tunnel leading deep into the pyramid.

"Be careful," said Louise. "My library book told me that the people who made the pyramids often put booby traps to stop tomb-robbers."

"I don't like the sound of that," said Charlie.

"They just say that to scare us

off," said Medhi. "It's perfectly safe."

Frankie heard a scurrying sound ahead. "Is that you, Max?" he asked.

"Nope," said his dog.

"Then I don't like the sound of it either!" whispered Charlie.

"Just relax," said Medhi. "It's just scarab beetles, and maybe the odd scorpion."

"And that's supposed to make us relax, is it?" said Max. "No wonder you're following up at the rear."

Frankie heard a faint *click*, then . . .

WHOOSH!

A shape shot through the

darkness straight towards Max, who froze. Charlie dived and stretched out an arm. The object rebounded into a wall with a crash. As the dust cleared, Frankie saw it was a stone football.

"Nobody move!" said Frankie.

No more balls came whizzing through the air. Frankie slowly

crouched by Max's side. "Lift your paws one at a time," he said. As Max obeyed, Frankie saw a stone button under his left front paw, almost hidden under a coating of sand.

"Our first booby trap," said Frankie.

"Let's go back," said Charlie. "It's too dangerous."

As he turned, Medhi blocked his way, raising a pick-axe threateningly. "I don't think so," he said. "We're going to find that mask, or die trying."

"I knew we shouldn't have trusted you," said Louise.

Frankie's anger swelled, but

he tried to keep a clear head. He looked at the stone ball that had almost squished Max. There could be dozens of them hidden away, ready to shoot out.

"I've got an idea!" he said. He reached over and picked up the heavy ball.

Just what I need, he thought.

"Move it!" said the robber.

Frankie faced the empty corridor, then drew back his arm like he was at the bowling alley. He sent the ball rolling straight down the centre of the passageway.

Click . . . click . . . clickety . . . click . . .

As the stone football bobbled over more hidden switches, stones shot from the walls like cannonballs. Some thumped into the ground, while others rebounded off the walls. Some collided and smashed each other to dust.

Slowly the cloud of debris settled.

"Good thinking!" said Charlie. "You set off all the traps."

Frankie breathed a sigh of relief. "Let's go," he said.

They set off through the rubble, making sure they walked exactly where the ball had rolled.

"So who else is on King Tut's

team?" said Louise. "We only saw him with a girl."

"That's his sister, Princess Cleo," said Medhi. "The captain is King Tut's dad . . . the Menacing Mummy."

"A mummy?" asked Louise. "You mean, like a dead person wrapped in bandages?"

"Careful what you say," said Medhi. "He's very proud of his kit. King Tut's dad was football mad. He made sure that Tut practised every day."

"Who's the fourth player?" asked Charlie.

Medhi grinned uneasily. "You probably don't want to know."

The passage became darker and darker, until soon Frankie could see barely five paces ahead. "At least there are no more flying footballs," muttered Max.

They heard a deep rumble.

"What's that?" said Medhi.

The rumbling grew louder, like approaching thunder.

"Uh-oh!" said Charlie, looking back.

Frankie glanced back too. A huge shadow was rolling towards them – a stone football as big as a car that completely filled the tunnel.

Medhi dropped his pick-axe and pushed Louise out of the way. He

took off down the passage at top speed.

"I don't think I can save *that*!" said Charlie.

"After Medhi!" said Frankie.

Barely looking where he was going, Frankie sprinted down the passage. The ground shook beneath his feet. *One trip and I'll be a human pancake.*

But the passage seemed to go on forever. Frankie checked over his shoulder and saw the ball was picking up speed. He saw Medhi just ahead, throwing back panicked glances. Then he stopped.

"Dead end!" he cried.

Frankie spotted dim light at the side of the tunnel. *Another passage.*

"In there!" Frankie pointed.

Louise skidded to a halt and jumped into the narrow gap. Charlie went after her, then Max. Frankie followed, squeezing his body through.

"Wait for me!" yelled Medhi. But he was too big. He couldn't fit. The ball kept coming and the robber looked terrified. "Don't leave me!" he begged.

Frankie grabbed Medhi's arm. With a tug, he heaved him through the gap just as the crushing boulder careered past and slammed into the wall ahead. It blocked the passage completely.

"You saved my life!" said Medhi.

Frankie wiped the sweat out of his eyes and took in the chamber around them. It was a square, and a smouldering torch rested in a metal loop above the door they'd come through. The room was completely bare apart from another stone football in the centre. Louise did a quick circuit. "We're trapped!" she said. "There's no way out."

Max did the same, sniffing. "She's right."

Frankie took the torch from the

wall and ran it along the walls, looking for a hidden doorway. Nothing. But as he lifted the torch to the far wall, he saw it wasn't bare like the others. It was covered in carved symbols in neat columns and rows.

"Hieroglyphs!" said Charlie, proudly. "What do they say?"

Medhi looked at his feet. "I'm afraid I can't read."

"There must be a way out," said Frankie. He touched the wall. It didn't feel as cold as he expected. "It's not stone," he said. He rapped it with his knuckles and heard a hollow sound. "Wood!"

"I'll get us out," said Medhi. "Let's throw the ball at the wall and smash through it. Stand back, everyone!"

"Are you sure this is a good idea?" began Louise.

Medhi picked up the ball, and at the same moment dust showered down from the ceiling.

Then the roof began to inch closer.

"What have you done now?" Max whined. "You've set off another trap."

Medhi hurled the ball at the wooden wall, but it didn't even make a dent.

The ceiling shifted again, pressing down.

It's going to crush us! thought Frankie.

Medhi picked up the ball and threw it again with the same effect.

"I think we need a Plan B," he said.

CHAPTER 5

Keep calm, Frankie told himself. He tried to ignore the ceiling edging ever closer as he peered at the hieroglyphs. But what hope did he have? He couldn't read them any better than the tomb-robber who'd brought them here.

One line of symbols, right in the

centre, caught his attention. They looked ancient, like the others, but somehow different. These three little drawings showed a man in various positions with a round object.

"He's playing football!" said Frankie.

Louise came to his side. "I think I know how to get out," she said. "You have to match the pictures!"

Frankie looked again. In the first picture the figure was balancing the ball on his right foot. In the second on his left. In the third he was bent over, with the ball behind his head, resting on the back of his neck.

But with a stone ball . . . ?

"Better do something quick,"
said Charlie, pointing upwards.
The ceiling was three metres up
and pressing further down by the
second.

Frankie snatched the ball off
the ground and rolled it onto his
right foot. It was so heavy he could
hardly hold it. He flicked the ball up
a fraction and tried to catch it on
his left. It rolled off.

"No time for nerves," said Max.
"Come on, Frankie!"

Frankie brought the ball back
onto his right foot. He tossed it to
his left foot. This time he managed
to cushion the ball. Almost straight

away his left leg started to tremble with the weight.

"Get on with it!" cried Medhi. He began to crouch as the ceiling touched his hair.

Then the torch went out, and everything went dark.

Frankie took a deep breath. He'd done the trick a hundred times with a normal ball, but never in the dark. *If I get it wrong, I'll crack my skull.* He grunted as he jerked his foot upwards and then bent at the waist to stoop beneath the ball. He felt the ball land on the back of his neck and wobble. Frankie manoeuvred for balance.

At the same moment, the wooden wall cracked open in the centre, flooding the room with light. The ceiling kept descending.

"You did it!" shouted Louise.

Blinking, Frankie let the stone ball drop to the ground and followed the others as they barrelled through towards the light.

As his vision cleared, Frankie gasped at the sight below.

They stood on a balcony, high above an enormous square chamber lined with stone seats, all sloped like the outside of the pyramid. A thin shaft of light came through a hole in the roof, casting a line of shadow across the arena. Two goals, marked with stone posts, stood at opposite ends. All around the outside of the pitch area were figures of men and women in football poses – reaching, kicking, stretching. *Weird,* thought Frankie. All that was missing from each statue was the football.

"This wasn't in my history books," said Louise, mouth gaping.

"For the last time, will the challengers please step forward?" said a man far below, in the centre of the arena. Though he wore long black robes, and his head was shaved to a shine, Frankie recognised the Ref. He had a whistle hanging round his neck. "Otherwise," he continued, "the match is forfeit and the Menacing Mummy wins."

"We're here!" called Frankie without even thinking. Everyone turned to face them and boos rippled through the chamber.

"You guys aren't very popular!" said Medhi, ducking back out of sight. "See ya!"

"At last!" said the Ref. "And what do you call yourselves?"

"Frankie's Fantasy FC," cried Louise.

The boos and hisses intensified,

echoing off the stone walls.

The Ref held out his hands towards a set of golden doors behind him. "And where are our champions?" he bellowed.

The crowd all shot to their feet at once, and began to chant "KING TUT! KING TUT! KING TUT!"

Through the gateway came the boy Frankie had seen before. His sister with the straight fringe was trying to walk beside him, but he kept skipping in front, as if he wanted to lead the way. They pushed and pulled at each other as they entered the arena.

But behind them came something

that made Frankie's skin crawl. A giant snake slithered across the sandy ground. Its mouth was big enough to swallow Max.

"Something tells me that *thing* is on their team," said Max.

The snake had a rope tied over its neck and it dragged something very familiar. A huge oblong coffin, painted in bright colours and gold leaf.

"It's the sarcopha-thingy from the museum!" said Charlie.

The Ref edged cautiously towards the coffin and unfastened two clasps on the side. Crouching down, he pushed the lid open with a creak. Frankie, along with everyone else in the arena, found himself leaning forward. Inside the coffin lay a figure wrapped in bandages, completely still.

"It's the mummy!" whispered Louise.

The Ref stepped back, quaking. "Arise!" he called.

For a moment, nothing happened, and then the sound of a huge yawn came from the coffin. The mummy lifted one bandaged arm, and gripped the side.

He sat up slowly.

"He's alive!" said Max.

"That's impossible," said Louise.

As the mummy raised a leg to
climb out, he almost tripped. Tut
ran forward and gave him an arm to
lean on.

"Steady on, Dad," he said.
"You've had a long nap."

"Let's go," said Frankie. He led
the way down steep stone steps

until they reached the bottom. The mummy turned stiffly to face them. So did the snake. It opened its jaws wide to reveal long, dripping fangs.

"Theeee*sss* mu*sss*t be our opponent*sss*," it hissed.

King Tut puffed out his chest. "Shouldn't be a problem," he said.

Princess Cleo sneered, and the mummy let out a long moan. The crowd responded with a cheer.

The Ref reached into the open sarcophagus and took out a golden mask and a golden football. "The winner will take the mummy's mask!" he said, placing it carefully on top of the coffin lid.

That must be what Medhi wanted to steal, thought Frankie. *It certainly looks like it's worth a lot of money.*

The Ref pointed to the shadow, which moved slowly across the floor. "And the game will end when the shadow has crossed the pitch!" He brought his whistle to his lips.

"Ready?" Frankie said to his team.

Charlie and Louise nodded. Max wagged his tail.

The Ref blew the whistle and tossed the ball high into the air.

CHAPTER 6

Frankie ran for the ball, but so did King Tut. Frankie sprinted as fast as he could and got there a fraction before his opponent. He passed the ball out towards Louise. Cleo leapt from nowhere and blocked the pass.

"To me!" yelled her brother,

hopping up and down. "Give it to me!"

Cleo ignored him and ran towards Charlie's goal. Frankie could see she was lightning fast. Max tried to tackle her, but she dribbled past him.

"I want it!" cried Tut.

But Cleo wasn't giving the ball to anyone. Frankie ran towards her, keeping his eyes on the ball. Max was chasing her too. Cleo raised her foot to shoot . . .

Frankie slid across the ground, and knocked the ball away. Cleo ended up in a heap on the sandy ground.

"Why didn't you pass?" said her brother. He looked at the mummy. "Dad! Tell her she shouldn't hog the ball."

The mummy groaned.

Frankie controlled the ball and kicked a short pass to Louise. "Let's stay close," he said. "That girl Cleo is quick."

Louise knocked the ball to Max. "Sure thing, Frankie."

As the dog turned, he came face-to-face with Viper. The snake's eyes gleamed like black glass. "What'*sss* thi*sss* ta*sss*ty mor*sss*el?" he said.

Max skidded to a halt.

"Better watch out for Viper's venom," said Tut. "It turns people to stone."

Frankie gulped, looking around at the statues at the edge of the arena. *So they're not statues after all,* he thought. *They're ex-players!*

Max backed off and then dug his front paws beneath the ball. He chipped it over the snake's head and scampered around him.

Quick as a flash, Viper twisted around and stopped the ball with his tail, balancing it right on the tip. Then he flicked it in a loop right to the mummy's feet.

The mummy groaned.

"Doesn't say much, does he?" said Louise.

"He never did," said Tut, his face sulky. "All he did when he was alive was play football. And when he wasn't playing, he liked to watch football."

"Sounds like my dad," said Charlie. "He's glued to Sky Sports at the weekend."

The mummy moved slowly, wrapped in bandages.

I'll tackle him, no problem, Frankie thought.

But as he got closer, the mummy's feet became a blur of dummies and step-overs. Frankie tried to kick the ball, but he missed time and again.

"Go, Dad!" said Cleo. "Show them how it's done!"

The mummy blasted a shot at the goal, and Charlie dived low. He must have got a fingertip to the ball, because the shot bounced against the post and out again to Louise.

"Great save, Charlie!" said Frankie.

He noticed the shadow was moving quickly across the ground. It wouldn't be long until the game was over. Frankie had learned none of these matches were normal.

"Quick, Charlie!" said Frankie.

The goalie rolled the ball out to Frankie, who quickly turned and tried to run around the lumbering mummy. But the bandaged figure quickly side-stepped, blocking him. He tried the other way, but the mummy was there again. *It's like he can read my mind,* thought Frankie.

The arena was almost all in shadow. Frankie back-heeled the ball to Louise. He realised too late that Viper had seen the pass. It reared back, fangs dripping, but Louise hadn't seen it.

"Look out!" Frankie yelled.

Louise turned and saw the snake

darting its head at her, but she
seemed glued to the spot. Then
Charlie appeared, leaping through
the air. Venom shot from Viper's
fangs, straight into Charlie's gloves.
Straightaway, they thumped to the
ground and turned to stone. Charlie
ripped his hands free.

"You saved me!" said Louise.

"Always ready," gasped Charlie, blushing. "But what about my gloves?"

"What about the open goal?" Max barked.

The ball had rolled free. Both King Tut and Cleo dashed towards it.

Frankie sprinted forward too.

"It's mine!" yelled the boy.

"No, it *mine*!" snapped Cleo.

The mummy groaned, as if he was fed up with their squabbling. Quick as a flash, he shouldered Frankie aside and pounced on the ball and started to run at the goal.

One of his bandages was trailing free.

Frankie watched in helpless horror as the Mummy lifted his foot to shoot.

Then he stopped dead, snagged by his bandage. His foot swung through the empty air and he landed on his backside with a thump.

Frankie looked back and saw the other end of the bandage in Max's teeth. There was just a sliver of sunlight left. Frankie darted towards the ball, took a quick glance at the distant goal, and booted it as hard as he could.

As the ball arced across the arena, the crowd drew a deep breath. Frankie saw the Referee bringing the whistle towards his lips.

The ball landed right between the posts and bounced over the line.

PEEEEP!

The whistle blew and a second later Frankie felt Charlie leap onto his back.

"Supergoal!" he cried. Frankie fell to his knees and Louise piled on too. Max nudged his nose into the pile-up, yapping happily.

CHAPTER 7

"Frankie's team are the winners!"
said the Ref.

Cleo stamped her foot and
crossed her arms. "What did I tell
you?" she said to her brother. "*I*
should have been captain, not you!
Girls always make better leaders."

"If you passed the ball more

often, we might have stood a chance!" said Tut.

The mummy groaned and started to shuffle back to his sarcophagus.

"He's probably fed up with listening to you two," said Louise.

"And now for the prize!" said the Ref. "Wait a minute . . . Where is it?"

Everyone looked to where the mask had been. It was gone!

"Someone's stolen it!" said the Ref.

Frankie glanced around and saw a man in the front row, making for the steps. "Max!" he said, pointing. "Fetch!"

Max's ears pricked up and he dashed after the fleeing figure, fastening his teeth on the hem of his robe. With a ripping sound, it tore free.

Medhi, dressed in just his tunic, had the golden mask tucked into his belt.

"Ah . . . er . . . I can explain . . ."

The crowd began to boo as the two burly guards from outside gripped him by the shoulders.

"We need someone to help build a new pyramid," one said. "It should only take you twenty or thirty years."

As one of the guards dragged

him away, Medhi cried out. "You don't understand! I wasn't *stealing* it. I was looking after it. Safe-keeping. You can't be too careful with all these thieves around . . ."

His voice trailed off as he disappeared through a door.

The other guard handed the mask back to Frankie, lowering his eyes. "Sorry we didn't believe you were the away team," he said.

"Don't worry," said Frankie, turning over the heavy mask in his hands. It was beautifully moulded, with two holes for eyes. "We've had a fun adventure getting here."

"We almost got squashed twice!"

mumbled Charlie. "You call that adventure?"

Louise gave him an elbow in the ribs and he went quiet.

"Put the mask on, Frankie," she said.

"Why?" he asked.

"It's just a hunch I've got," she replied.

Frankie lifted the mask to his face and placed it against his skin. The gold was warm, and as soon as it touched his skin, his body felt weightless, like he was floating off the ground. Then, through the eye-holes, he saw he *was* floating off the ground. So were the others.

Charlie wheeled his hands in panic, and Max's paws scrabbled in the air.

Louise grinned. "I think we're going home," she said.

Faster and faster they rose through the air, high above the Ref and the crowd. Wind whistled in Frankie's ears as they shot towards the ceiling.

"We're not going to stop!" he yelled.

Have I made a terrible mistake?

He raised his hands to shield himself and closed his eyes.

BOOM!

Frankie felt solid ground under his feet and he swayed dizzily.

He opened his eyes and saw the Egyptian room at the museum. Charlie and Louise stood beside him. He was holding his magic football.

"You three!" bellowed a voice. They all spun around. Mr Donald stood in the doorway, smoke practically shooting from his ears. Beside him stood a woman with a museum nametag. "Ms Jones here told me there were children playing football in the museum," said their teacher. "Explain yourselves."

Frankie looked at the ball in his hands, then at Charlie and Louise.

Charlie shrugged – he was wearing his gloves again, and they weren't made of stone. Louise opened her mouth as if she was about to speak, then closed it again.

What can I possibly say?

"As I thought," said Mr Donald. "You three will be in detention next week. I might even have to write to your . . ."

"Oh my!" gasped Ms Jones. She ran from Mr Donald's side, straight past Frankie, and stopped at the rope beside the sarcophagus. "It . . . it can't be!"

Frankie drew a sharp breath. The coffin wasn't empty anymore.

Inside stood the golden mask, gleaming brightly.

"The mummy's mask!" said the museum worker. "But how . . . ? It's never been found!"

"I guess it has now," said Frankie.

Mr Donald had come in as well, and he was gaping at the mask.

Charlie leant close to Frankie's ear. "I think Donaldo's forgotten about detention," he whispered. "Maybe we should get back to the bus."

"Good idea!" said Frankie.

Acknowledgements

Many thanks to everyone at Little,
Brown Book Group; Neil Blair, Zoe
King, Daniel Teweles and all at The
Blair Partnership; Mike Jackson
for bringing my characters to life;
special thanks to Michael Ford
for all his wisdom and patience;
and to Steve Kutner for being a
great friend and for all his help and
guidance not just with this book but
with everything.